TOPSYS & TURVYS

BY PETER NEWELL

DOVER PUBLICATIONS, INC., NEW YORK

Published in Canada by General Publishing Company, Ltd., 30 Lesmill Road, Don Mills, Toronto, Ontario.

Published in the United Kingdom by Constable and Company, Ltd., 10 Orange Street, London W.C. 2.

This Dover edition, first published in 1964, consists of a selection made from the following books:

Topsys & Turvys by Peter Newell, as published by the Century Company in 1902.

Topsys and Turvys—Number 2 by P. S. Newell, as published by the Century Company in 1894.

International Standard Book Number: 0-486-21231-9
Library of Congress Catalog Card Number: 64-18861

Manufactured in the United States of America

Dover Publications, Inc.
180 Varick Street
New York 14, N.Y.

When Bertram Bowles fell off the dock, so loudly did he shout,

That Clarence Cowles leaned o'er the edge and hoisted Bertram out.

They heard a flock of booby-birds come whirring through the air.

Beneath their big and shady hats the bathers had a scare—

Here is a German farmer dressed in a curious rig,

And looking rather sad because he's lost his fattened pig.

Till—bang!—his magazine blew up, and hurled the crew in air.

The Malay pirate eyed his foes in hopeless fierce despair

"I'll come again," the small bird said, before the apple round;

But meanwhile came this greedy duck, and *she* the apple found.

The Storks, on seeing them, remarked, "It's time for us to go!"

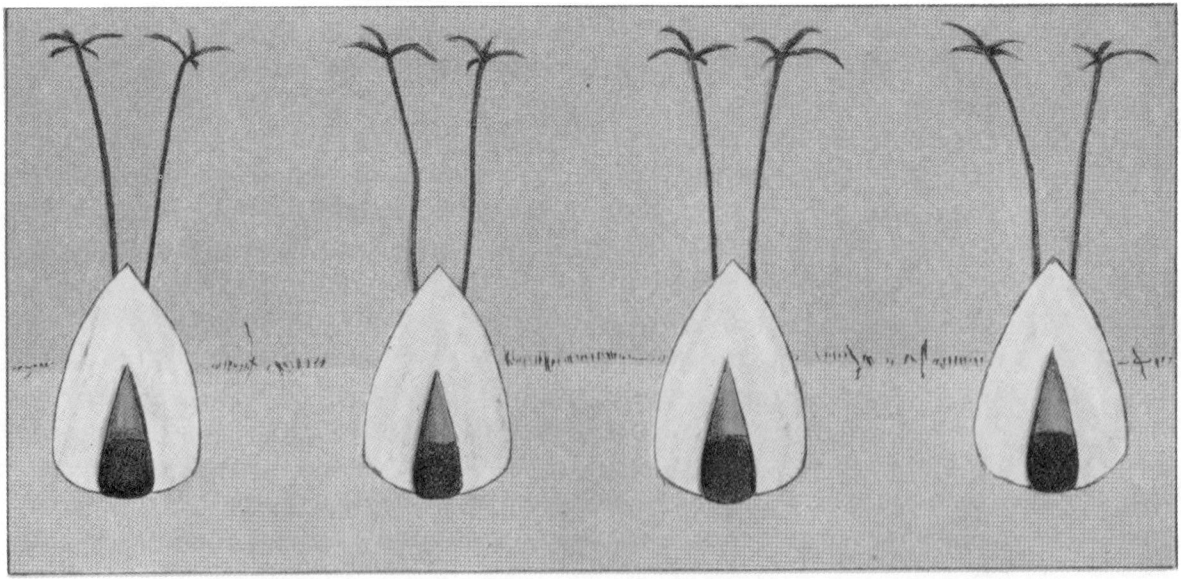

Beneath tall palms some Arabs pitched their tents as white as snow;

But, later on, in high fur cap, 't is thus that each appears.

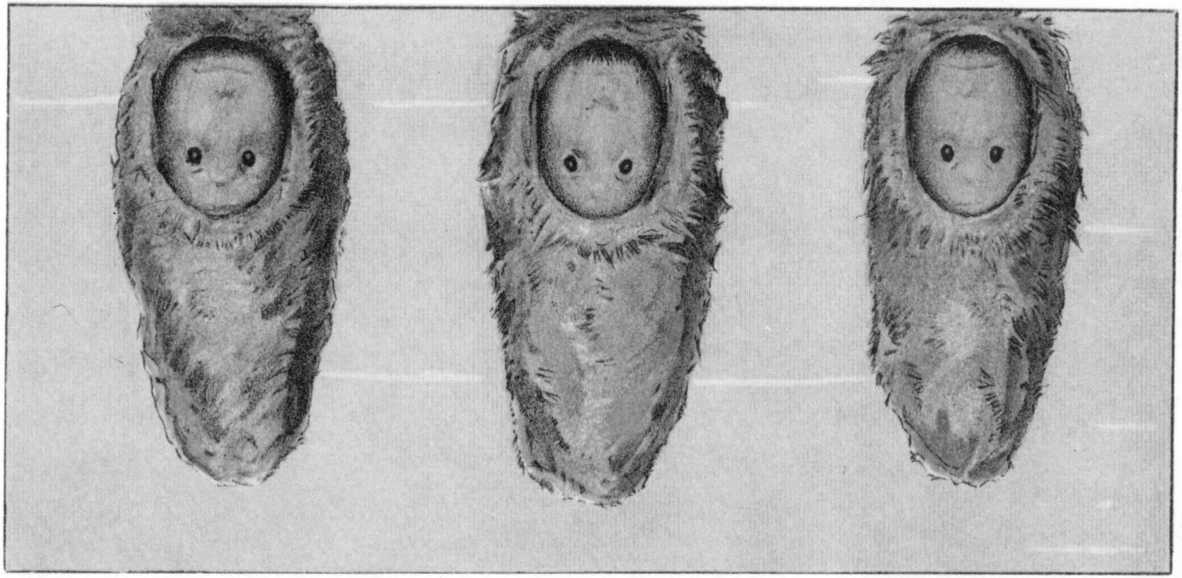

These innocent Papooses thus pass their early years,

Three frightened Citizens exclaimed, "My goodness! who are you?"

From three high hats three Jokers popped, all crying "Peek-a-boo!"

But by their clothes they saw a snake, when they came to the shore.

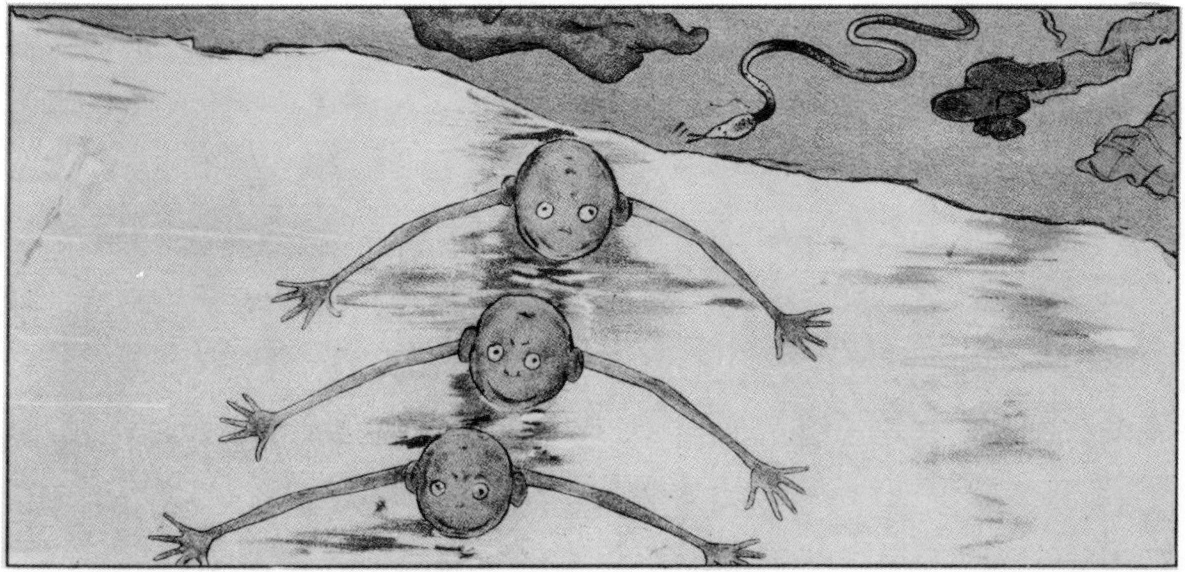

Three country boys went swimming, where oft they'd been before;

And upside down, upon their stalks, they took a little run.

The gardener set his choicest ferns where they would get the sun,

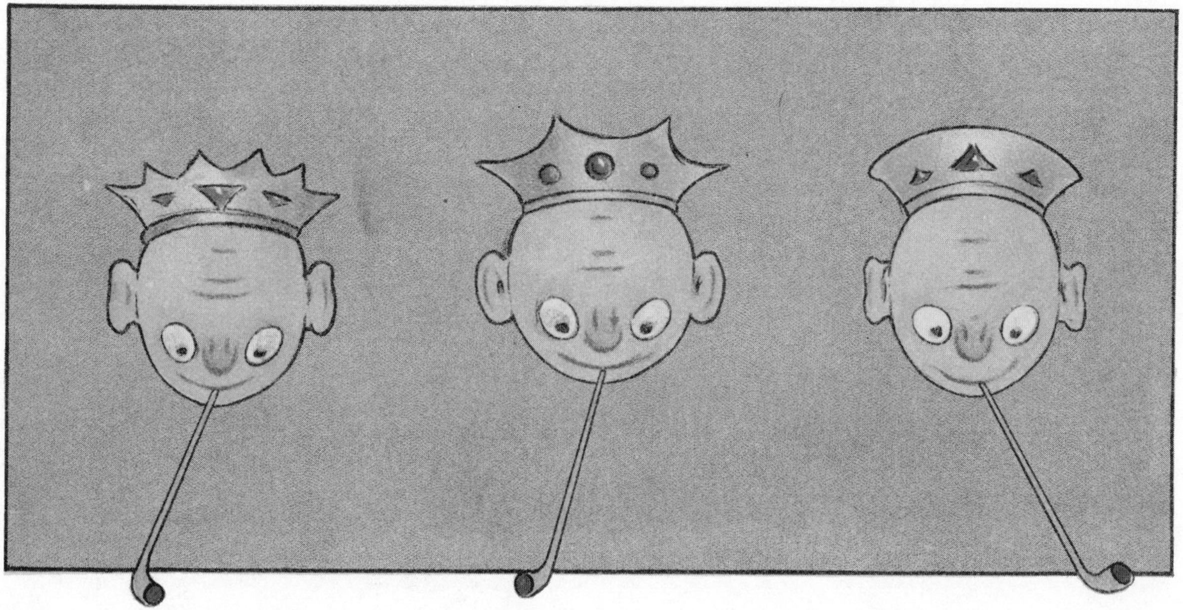

Three friendly Kings went to a show, and wore their pipes and crowns,

And there saw clever balancing by three accomplished Clowns.

But others claim this Duck was seen, and then the fact distorted.

Some say the famed Sea-serpent came, and by the shore disported,

Then the Banjo borrows Jerry's flute and plays a tune to him.

First young Jerry plays the banjo, and he twangs it with a vim,

"'I've hooked a fish!" cries hasty Hugh; "I'll land him, too. Now see!"

He gave a fling, and found the fish was hanging in a tree.

You see, it was a Spring lamb, and jumped the fence, no doubt.

The shepherd's looking for the lamb. "How did that lamb get out?"

He lost the gnat, but found this spring. It came up to his neck.

A broad-brimmed sage once chased a gnat, a tiny harmless speck.

And James Broadbrim, a Quaker slim, the same brave feat essays.

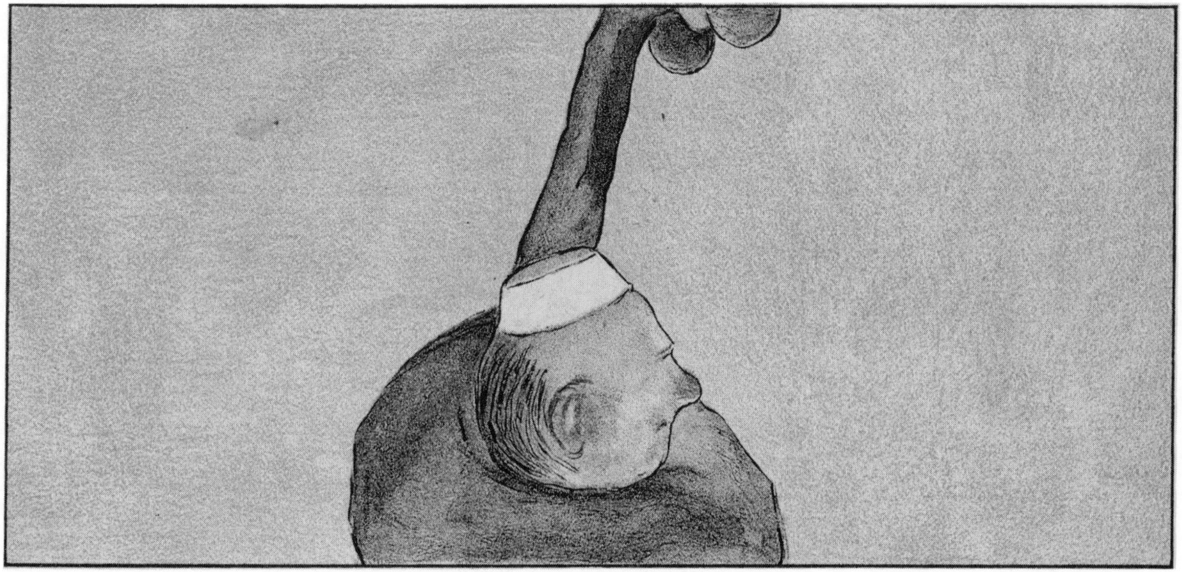

John Stout his tissues to reduce a dumb-bell thus does raise.

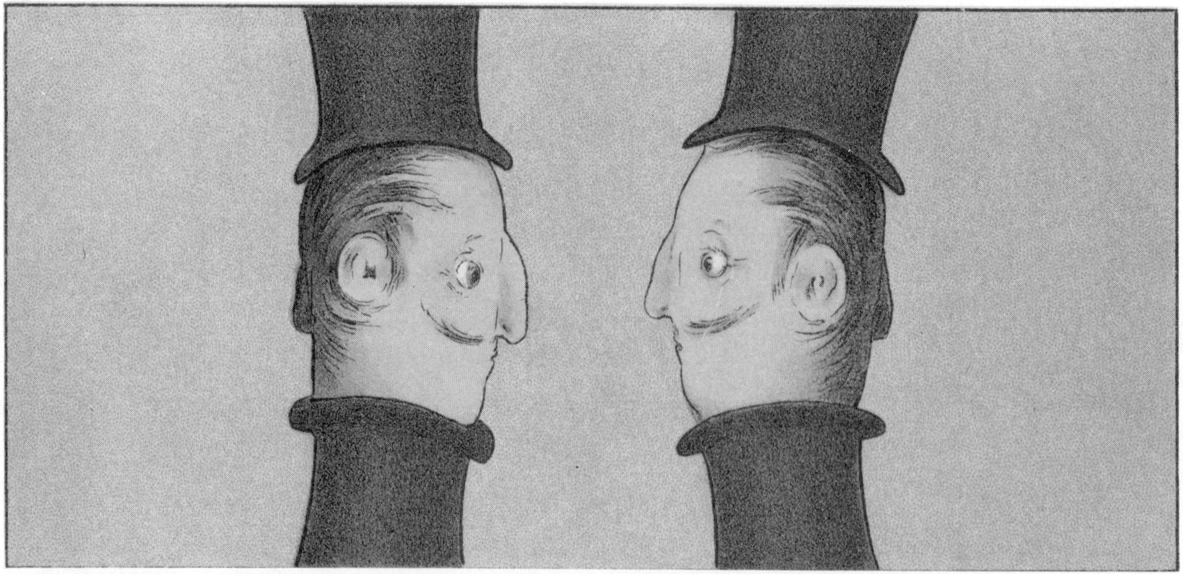

Two “chappies” on the avenue one foggy day did meet,

And side by side, with eye-glass fixed, they strolled along the street.

This shepherd thought poetic thoughts as by the flocks he sat;

But while he wrote his verses, the goat fed on his hat.

But in a tree the wildcat hid until he went away.

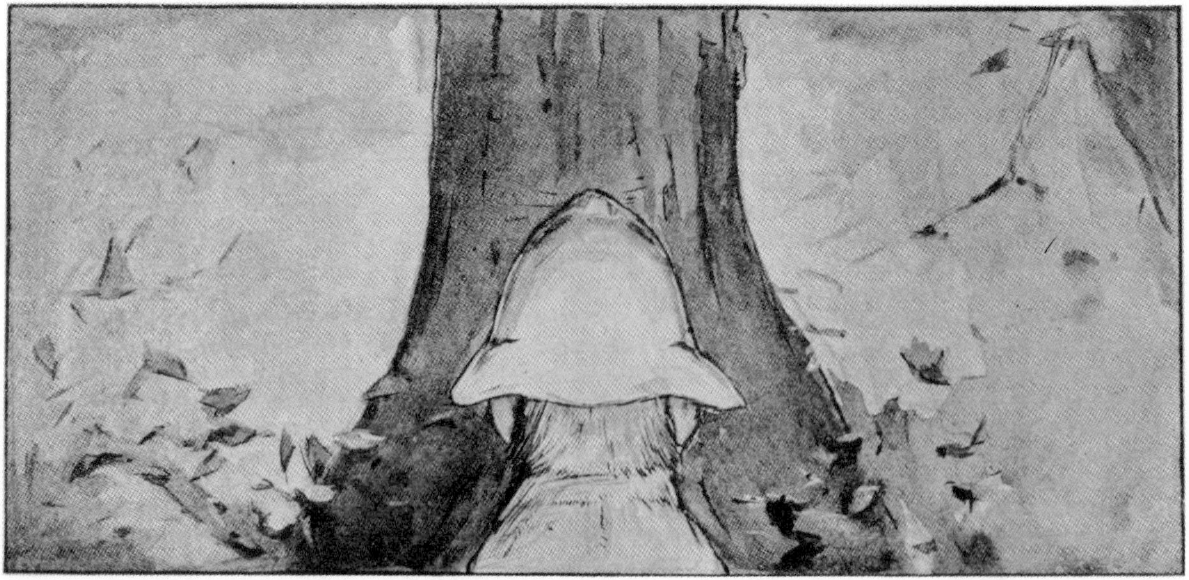

A hunter wandered through the wood in search of lurking prey;

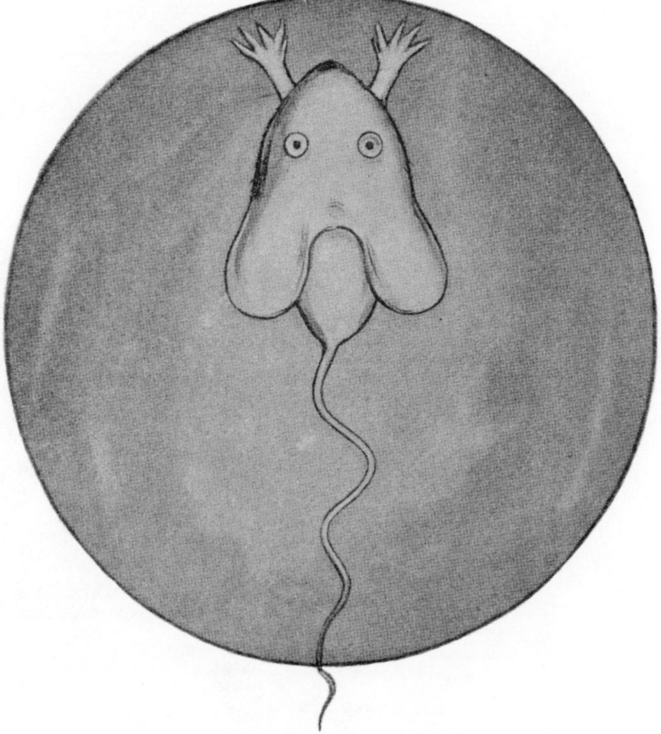

A drop of water magnified this creature queer reveals;

And look!—a microscopic mouse after the fellow steals!

Above his lair a hawk is perched, but poised for instant flight.

Hid in a nook the panther sleeps, and hunts for prey by night;

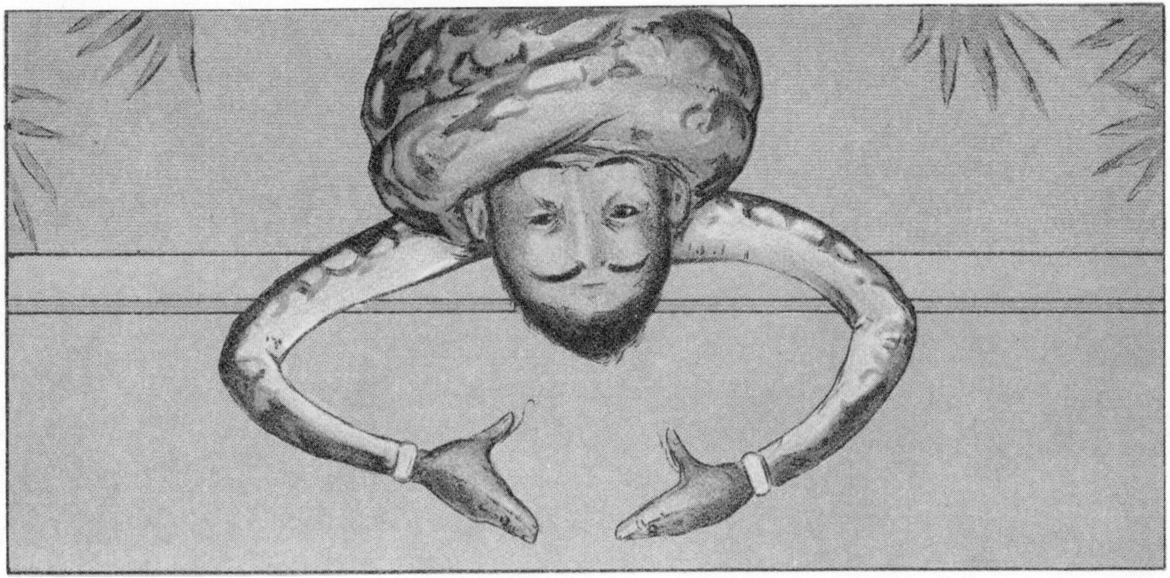

This is the serpent-charmer so brave he never quakes

When twice around his neck are wound two lively, squirming snakes.

Unto the dentist, who exclaims, "I'll take it out, of course!"

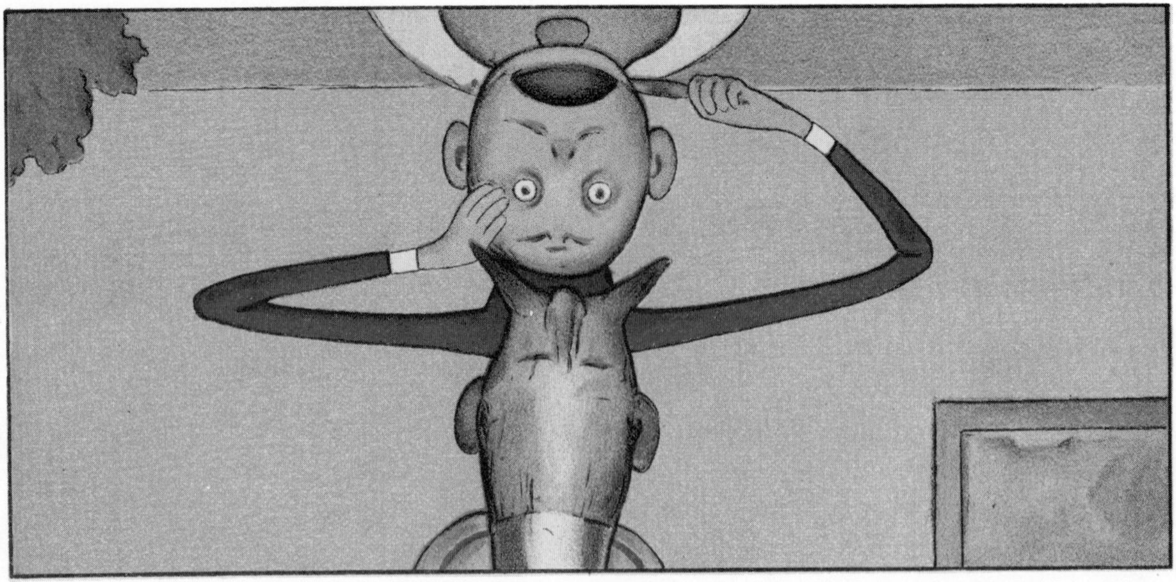

"Oh, my poor tooth!" the rider groans, and urges on his horse

They missed their aim, and not a bird of all the flock was caught.

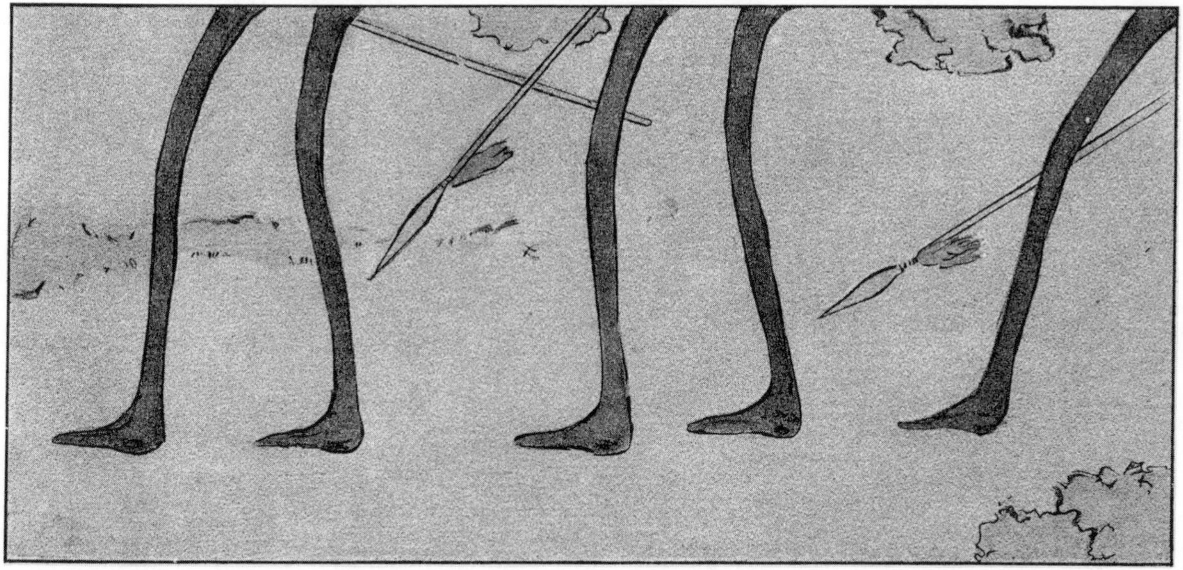

Some ostrich-hunters with their spears set out in search of sport;

Here are the fish they didn't catch, and now you may decide.

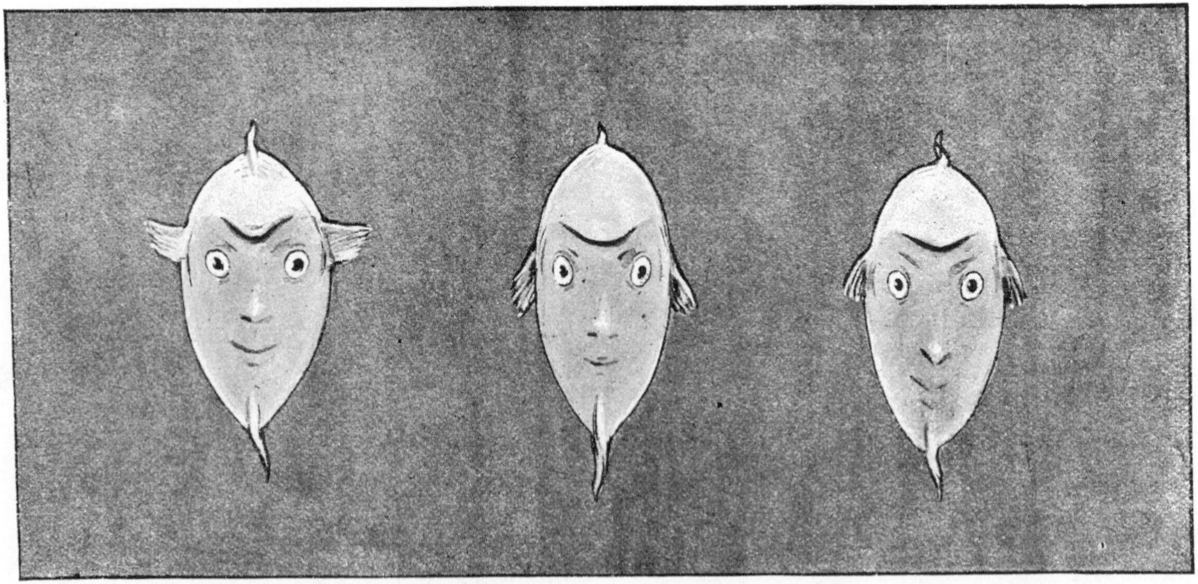

"The fish were bigger than our heads," they vowed,—"yes, twice as wide,"

Old Jerry wore his hat so long that it became a jest;

And then his old hen sat in it, and used it for a nest.

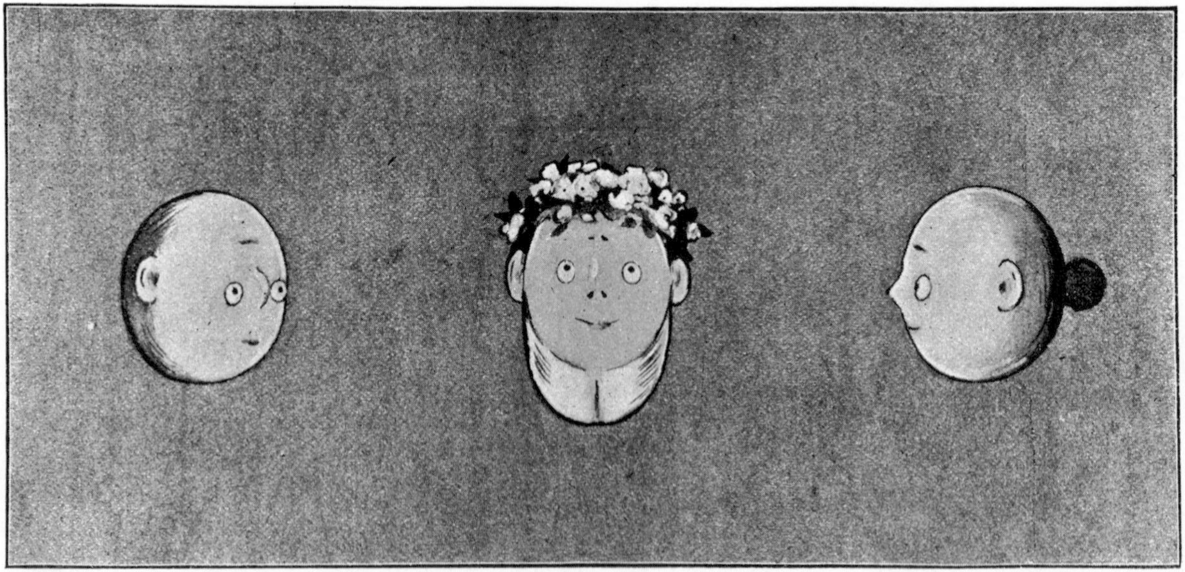

When on the May Queen's golden curls the pretty wreath was laid

It slipped down over head and ears, so large it had been made.

But when she sang a solo she did not look so sweet.

To singing-school Belinda went, a costume new and neat,

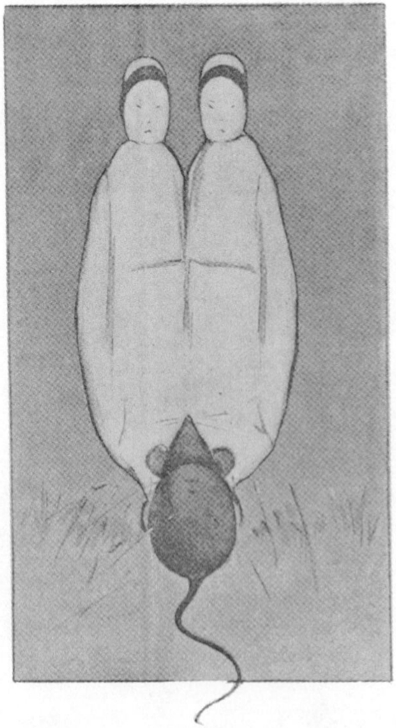

Two Chinese twins once met a mouse, and gazed on him with fright,

Till brave Ah Boo came toddling up and put the beast to flight.

When it's later, the spectator sees her hang her clothes to dry.

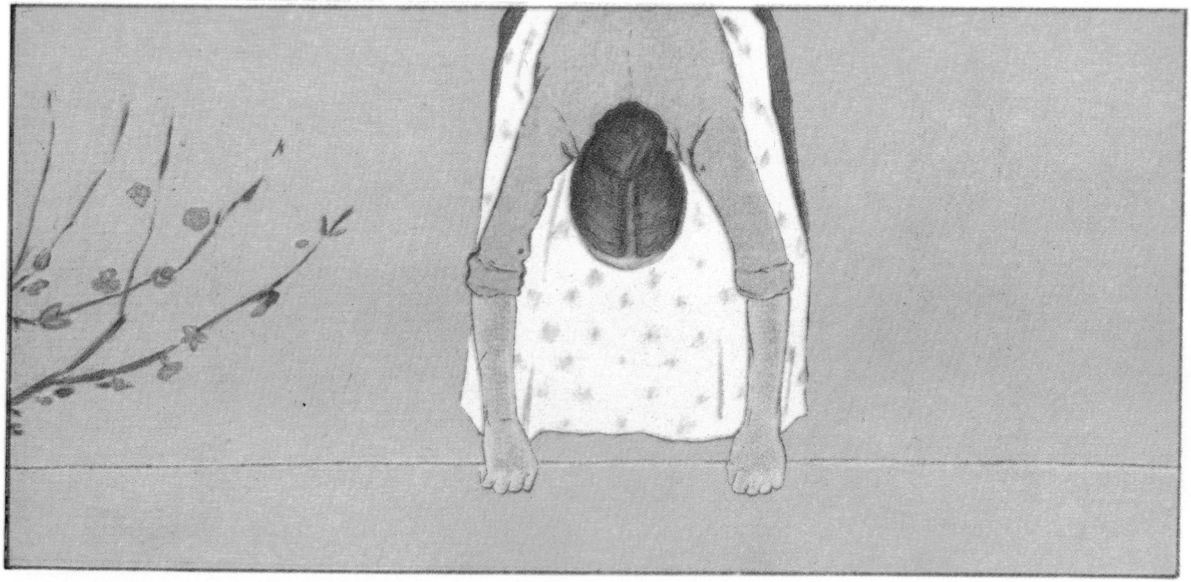

Rising early, Mrs. Burley in her garden meets the eye;

Because they know three hunting-dogs are close upon their trail.

Why do these scurrying, frightened hares come coursing through the vale?

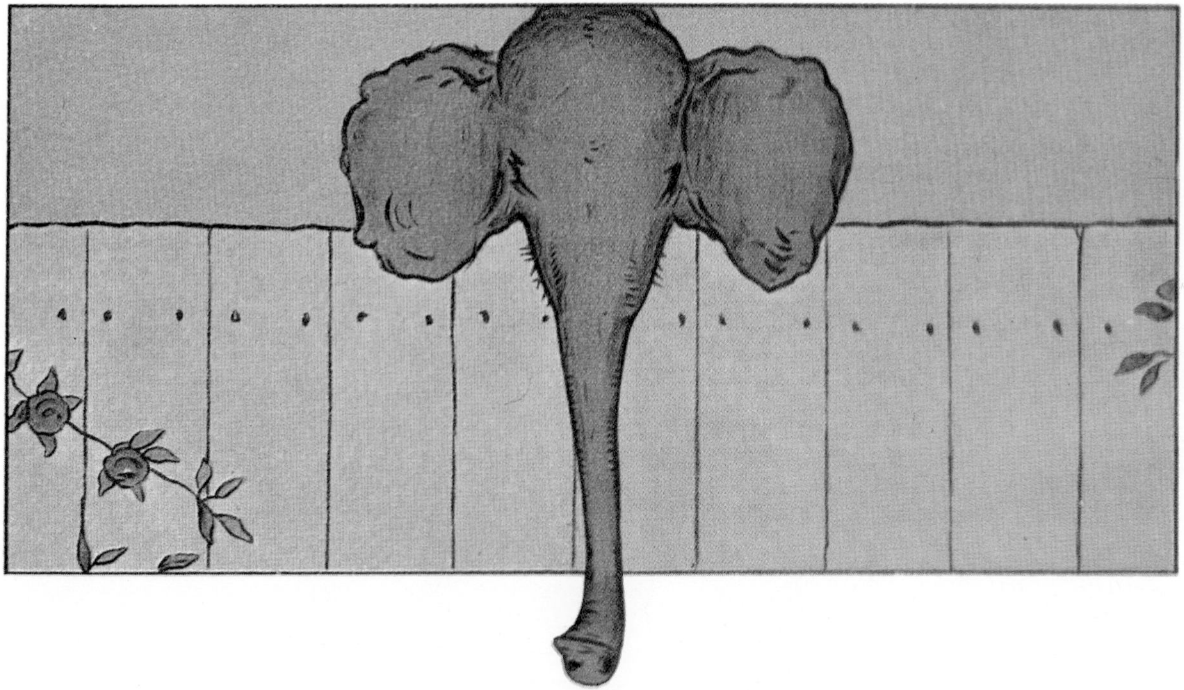

The Elephant leans o'er the fence and wonders why it is

The Ostrich has a longer neck and smaller mouth than his.

The squirrel gazed with wonder upon his gloomy face.

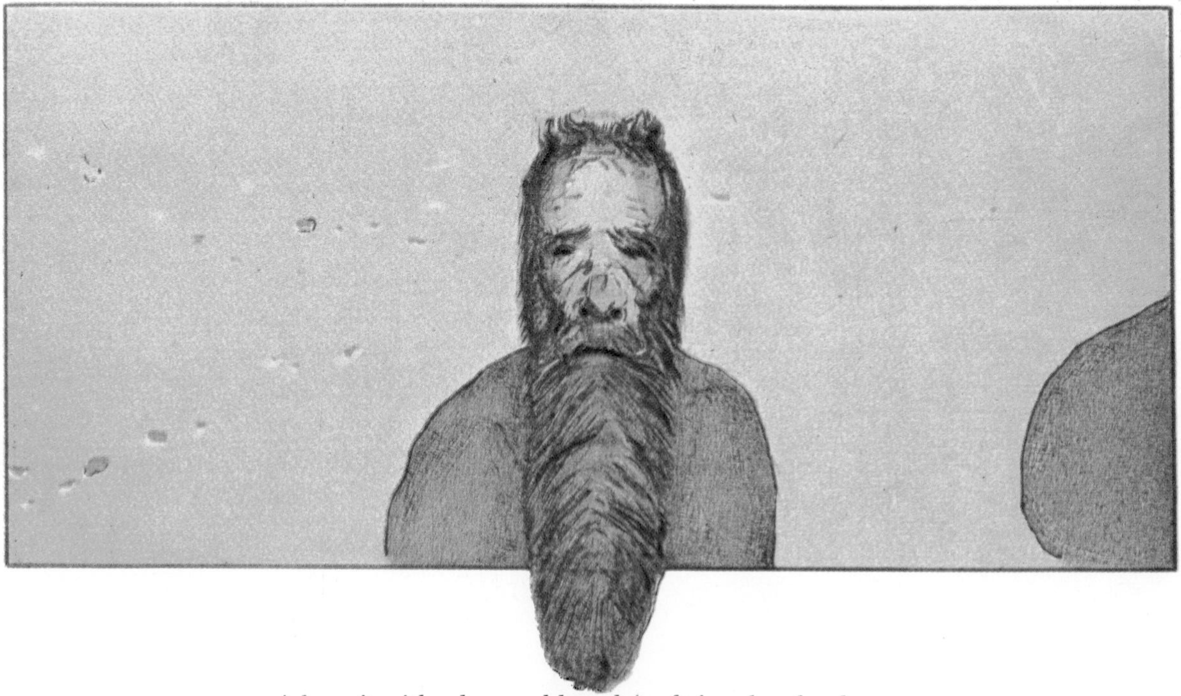

A hermit with a long red beard dwelt in a lonely place;

This troop of soldiers, all in file, are looking near and far

To find the famous Forty Thieves, each hid within a jar.

Fernando bears his cradle in, a cradle strong and deep,

Then, placing it upon a rug, he rocks himself to sleep.

A famous warrior of that land is ever in her head.

Here is a lady of Japan, and at the court, 't is said,

But Piggy smelled a rat (or wolf), and went another way.

In hope of pork, two small gray wolves watched all one autumn day;

The hunter found two bear-cubs and took them from their cave,

But when the mother bear returned, he fled his life to save.

Then everything is kicked in air, and kept there quite awhile.

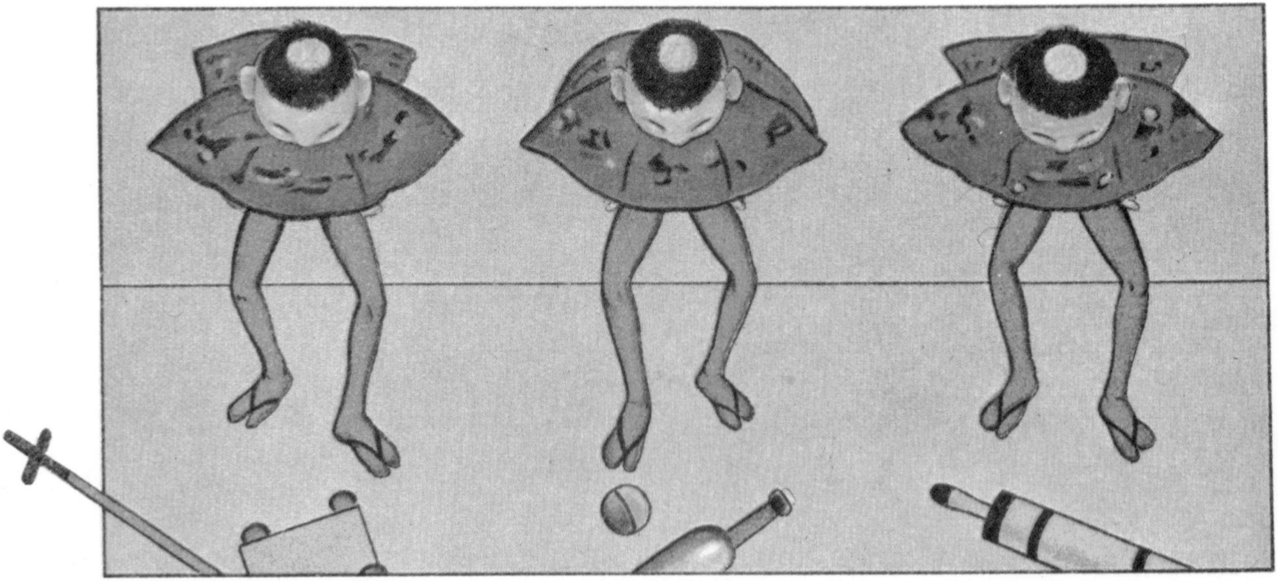

The juggling Japanese come out, they bow and sweetly smile,

But found the little manikin could well defend himself.

A wicked robber horseman charged upon a woodland elf,

Only his head and hands are seen, he sinks so very deep.

The rancher in the blizzard goes out to save his sheep,

When oh! a monster bird swooped down and seized him in its bill.

Within his skiff young Izaak sat, fishing with joy and skill,

But near the stream a long-legged stork secured a breakfast first.

Down to the river crawled a snake, meaning to quench his thirst;

Not like these shrieking parakeets, both spoiling for a fight.

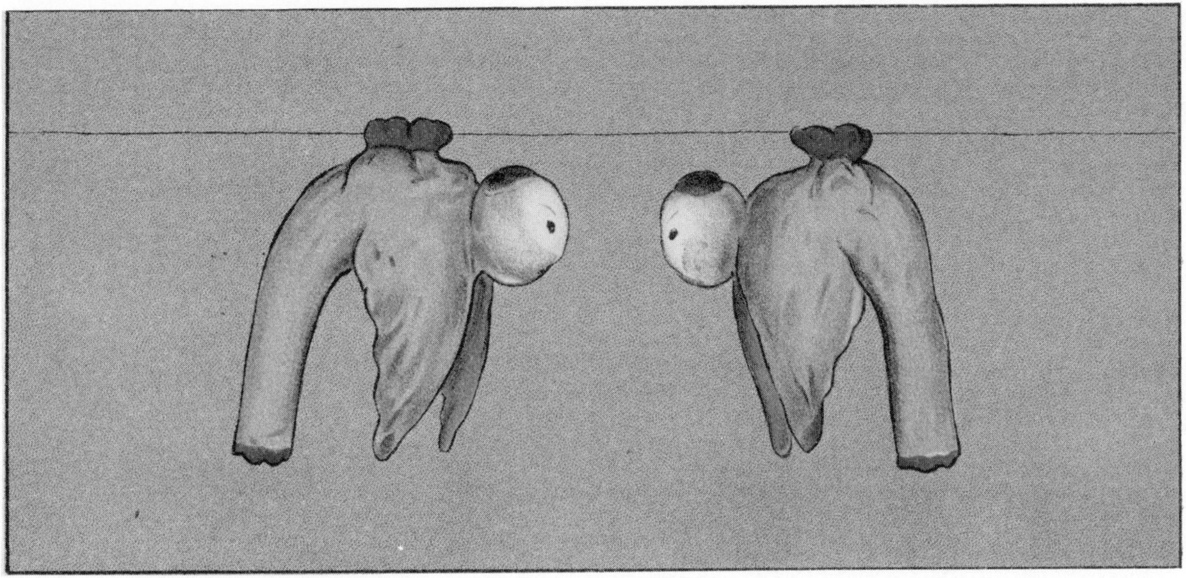

Upon a line, two Japanese, though dolls, are most polite;

The captain's pig fell overboard and swam with all his might,

Until the shark came gliding up, and put him out of sight.

But take to flight when on the bank rhinoceroses greet.

With cheerful caws two inky crows beside a river meet,

The people in the windows their keen amusement show,

To see these Jacks-in-boxes exhibited below.

And slides headforemost down the hill when Winter brings the snow.

In shady groves Adolphus swings when Summer's zephyrs blow,

While driving geese, and how they squawked to see Jan's pride thus humbled!

So clumsy were Jan's wooden shoes that in the pond he tumbled

Here's Uncle Ike, and Auntie Jane, the wife of Uncle Ike,

But which is which? It seems to me they're very much alike.

"Meow-meow! Pfitz-pfitz!—at me," says Mrs. Bulger's cat.

"Bow-wow! Wow-woof!" says Bulger's dog. What is he barking at?

And in their town the Woollyheads with fierce defiance shout.

The British fire a volley, behind their strong redoubt;

Until their nurse, kind Hannah, comes, to rock them both to sleep.

The patient twins are waiting within their cradle deep

His fine long-eared retriever plunged in and quickly got it.

A duck came flying o'er the pond; and when the sportsman shot it,

Three Merry Minstrels passing by were for their purses asked.

Three Robbers strode into the road, and each of them was masked.

I stood upon my head and saw this strange two-headed freak;

But, on my feet again, I saw this Owl so wise and meek.

Whether the musk-ox wears his horns in a becoming fashion.

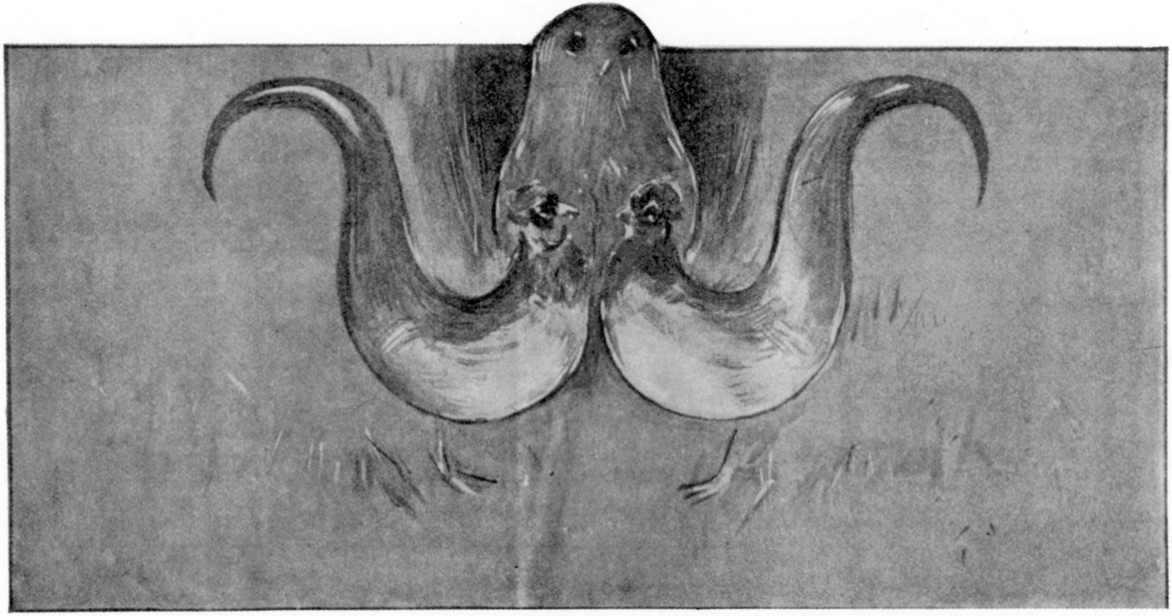

The owl looks on while fowls discuss till both are in a passion

But when he comes to speak his piece just see what animation!

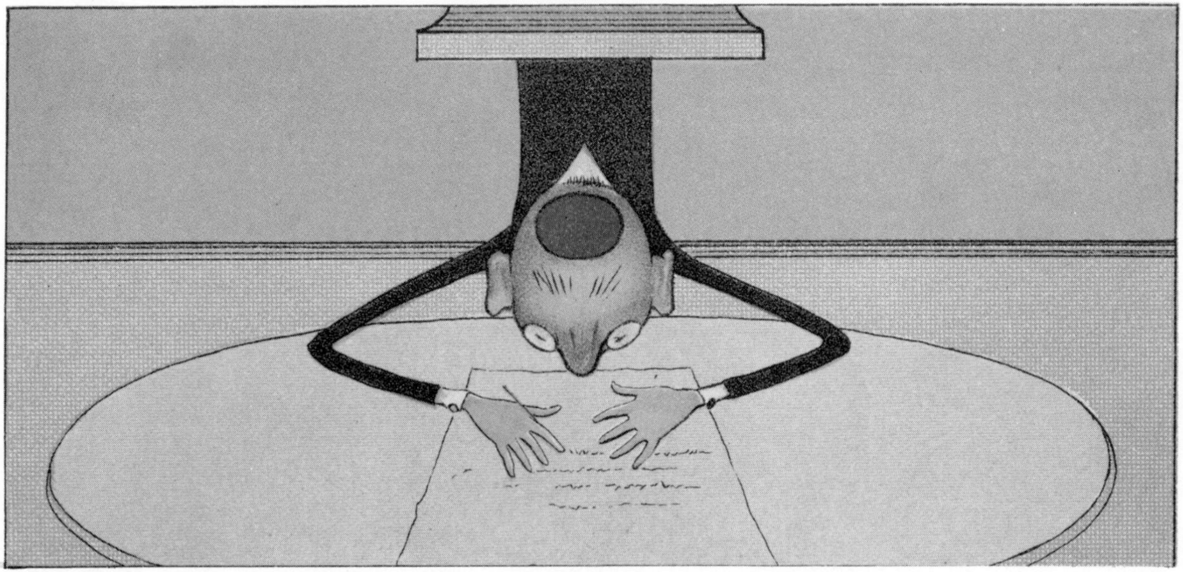

How quietly this learned Man writes out his great oration,

"I sent him off upon a lark; he won't be back to-day."

"Where is your son, now, Captain Blobbs? I hear he is away."

He plumps a big one in his mouth, and finds it very good.

The hungry tramp has come upon some cherries in the wood;

"I saw a pretty boy, but not like you that I could see."

"Oh, have you seen my little boy?—he looks not unlike me."

But when they linger by the sea they tan as brown as berries.

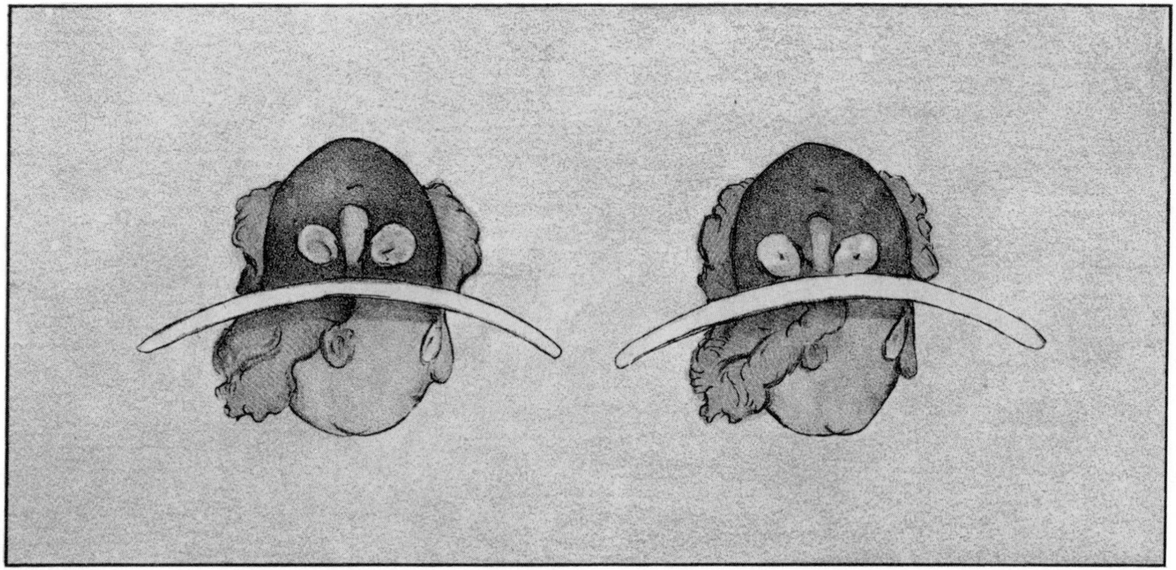

In town the Hickson girls are fair, with lips as red as cherries;

Jack Frost has nipped the leaves and brought the acorns tumbling down.

The acorns now are falling—the leaves are turning brown;

But finds it is a customer who says: "Please cut my hair."

At sight of this forbidding tramp, the barber has a scare,

So low that Rudolph couldn't get down to it at all.

They played a match at tennis, and Charlie served the ball

"You're flat!" remarked the buffalo, and left him with a sneer.

A tree-toad, perched upon a tree, was piping loud and clear;

The twins their Tam o' Shanters don, jump in and off they ride.

Before the house a cart is seen, a hat hung at each side.

But three fierce Dogs came growling out and drove them far away.

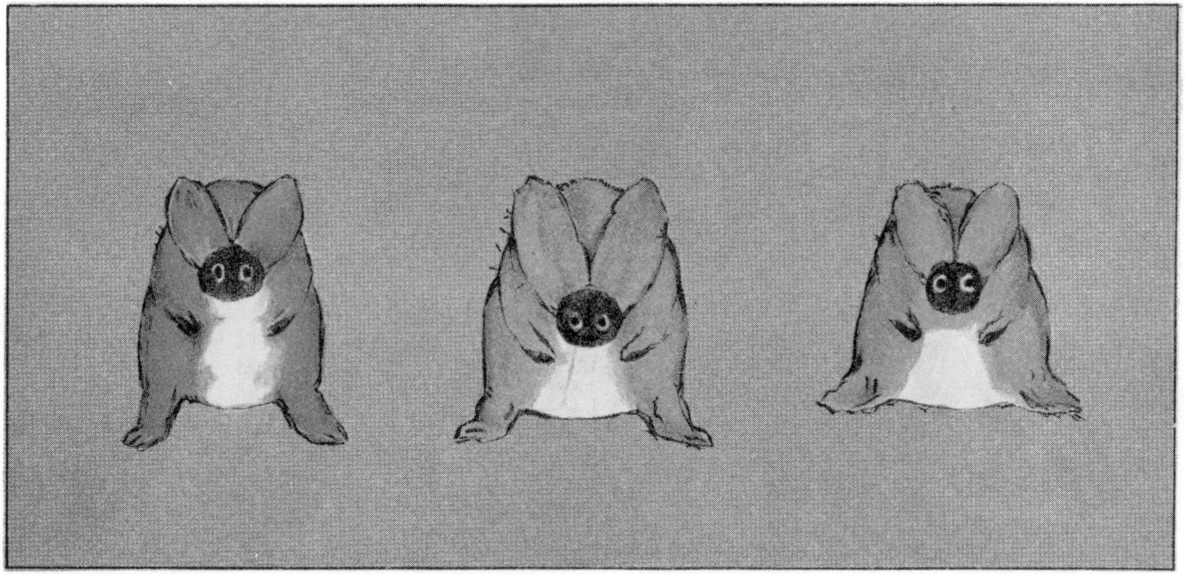

Three tender-hearted Wollypogs upon a lawn did play—,

A lion made an end of her—she came too near the shore.

The swan was swimming on a stream where oft she'd been before.

A foreigner in curious clothes sat resting in the shade,

While, just behind, a countryman undue surprise displayed.

And here's the awful thing they found—a donkey munching leaves.

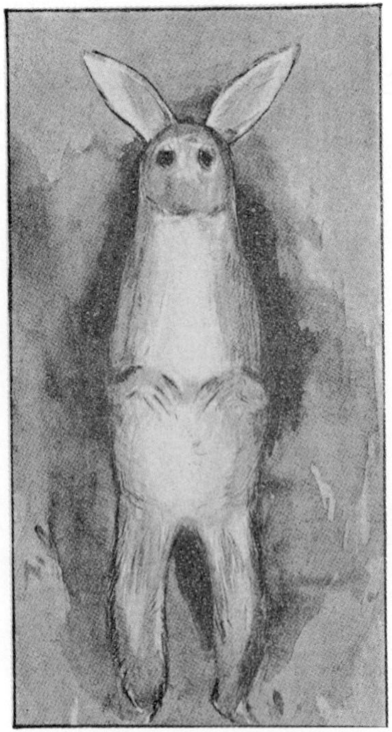

"I hear a noise!" the hare exclaimed. "Oh—murder, fire, *thieves*!"

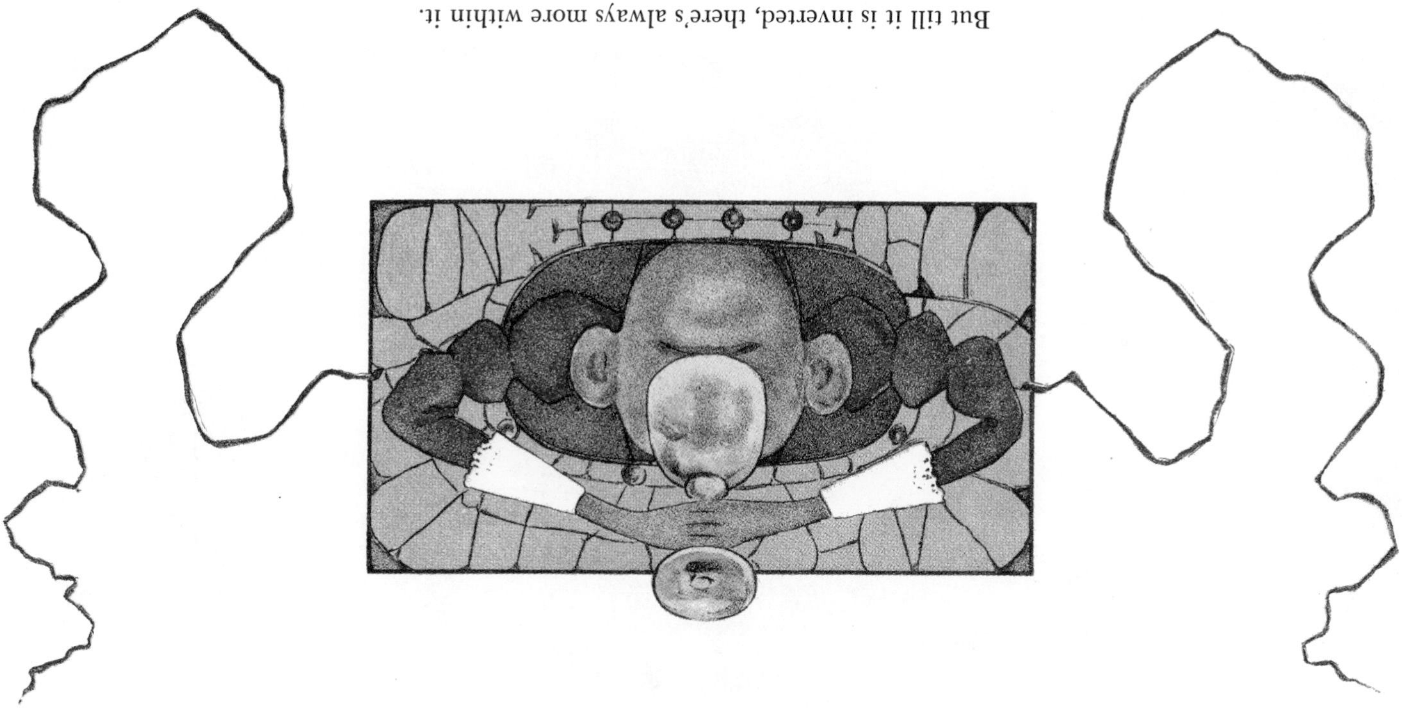

This book is like a tumbler. It's thus that you begin it,

But till it is inverted, there's always more within it.

We find the ending of this book in plainest text asserted.

And now appears a mystic word, but if it be inverted,